W9-BSL-831

DATE DUE

SEP 0 1 2020	
OCT 1 3 2020	

For Bingley, the original Dog —N.B.

Thank you to all the good boys, good girls, and domesticated pumas who helped me figure out these characters —A.Z.

Text copyright © 2020 by Nelly Buchet
Illustrations copyright © 2020 by Andrea Zuill
All rights reserved. Published in the United States by Schwartz & Wade Books,
an imprint of Random House Children's Books, a division of Penguin Random House LLC, New York.
Schwartz & Wade Books and the colophon are trademarks of Penguin Random House LLC.
Visit us on the Web! rhcbooks.com
Educators and librarians, for a variety of teaching tools, visit us at RHTeachersLibrarians.com
Library of Congress Cataloging-in-Publication Data
Names: Buchet, Nelly, author. | Zuill, Andrea, illustrator. Title: Cat dog dog / Nelly Buchet; Andrea Zuill.
Description: New York: Schwartz & Wade Books, [2020] | Summary: "A story of a blended family—from the pets' point of view!"—Provided by publisher.
Identifiers: LCCN 2019010263 | ISBN 978-1-9848-4899-4 (hardcover) | ISBN 978-1-9848-4900-7 (hardcover library binding)
| ISBN 978-1-9848-4901-4 (ebook)
Subjects: | CYAC: Dogs—Fiction. | Cats—Fiction. | Pets—Fiction. | Stepfamilies—Fiction.
Classification: LCC PZ7.1.B818 Cat 2020 | DDC [E]—dc23
The text of this book is set in Mr. Eaves Modern
The illustrations were rendered in ink, compiled digitally, and colored in Photoshop.
MANUFACTURED IN CHINA
10 9 8 7 6 5 4 3 2 1
First Edition

Cat Dog Dog

The story of a blended family

Words by Nelly Buchet

Art by Andrea Zuill

schwartz & wade books · new york

Dog

Dog

Dog

Dog

Dog   **Cat**

Dog Cat

Dog Cat

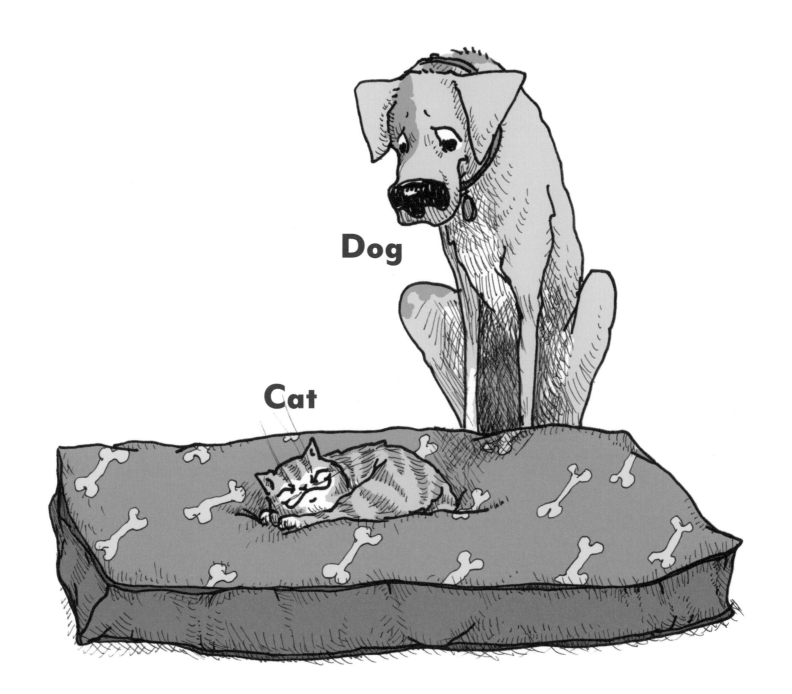

Dog Cat

Cat Dog Dog

Dog Cat Dog

Dog Cat

Dog

Bedroom

Bath

Dog

Dog Box

Dog Box

Dog Bo

Dog Dog

Dog Dog

Dog Dog

Cat Dog Dog

Cat

Dog Cat Dog

Bird

Dog Dog Cat

Cat

Dog Cat

Dog Dog

Dog Cat Dog

Dog Dog Cat   **Frog**

Dog Dog Cat

Dog Dog Cat

Cat Dog Dog

Dog Dog Cat

Dog Dog Cat